By: G. Scott Gibson

Illustrated by:
Arianna Gentile Polese

Halo ●●●●
Publishing International

ISBN 13: 978-1-935268-95-6
Library of Congress Control Number: 2012903440

Printed in the United States of America

Halo ● ● ● ●
Publishing International
www.halopublishing.com

Published by Halo Publishing International
AP·726
P.O. Box 60326
Houston, Texas 77205
Toll Free 1-877-705-9647
www.halopublishing.com
www.holapublishing.com
e-mail: contact@halopublishing.com

This book is dedicated to my beautiful children: Lyndie, Torrie, and Glenn. Also, to my parents who have always supported my crazy endeavors. Finally, to my English teachers who planted the seeds of confidence in my writings and encouraged me to keep dreaming.

- Scott

Torrie Mae Twiddle was sitting in class,
yesterday was her 9th birthday and she had a big birthday bash;
It was a "pink" birthday party with pink balloons and pink toys,
pink streamers, pink tables, ten girls and no boys.
They ate pink cake with pink frosting, pink ice cream and pink punch,
pink candies, pink mints, and pink cookies to crunch.

As Torrie Mae Twiddle was thinking about her party yesterday,
her stomach started bubbling and gurgling in a most horrible way.
A huge gas bubble formed and stretched her tummy real tight,
it started on her left side, and then moved to her right.

Her tummy was sloshing and squishing and shaking like a leaf
Torrie needed to leave the classroom to seek some relief.
She stepped out of the classroom where she had nothing to fear
And looked up and down the hallway to make sure the coast was clear.

Ms. Whoopie

Squeeek!

Torrie slowly lifted her left leg and put all of her weight on her right,
and started pushing out the giant gas bubble with all of her might.
Her tummy started tightening, her face started to scrunch,
her eyes started squinting and her back started to hunch.
Her bottom started rumbling like it had never done before,
it rattled the hall windows and shook the classroom doors.
There was a hiss of a snake and a growl of a bear,
a laugh of a hyena and a car tire losing its air.
A screech of an owl and a grunt from a hog,
A "boing" from a spring and a bark of a dog.
There was a squeak of a mouse and a scream of a monkey
And suddenly, ……………Torrie's tummy no longer felt so funky.

She turned herself around to go back into class,
when she noticed a huge thick, pink cloud of gas.
It was 3 feet wide and 5 feet tall,
a giant pink smokescreen that filled up the hall.

Torrie started to panic, her face frozen with fear
she couldn't believe this pink toot had come from her rear.
Torrie waved her hands quickly, fanning the pink toot away,
but the pink toot remained together; and wanted to stay.

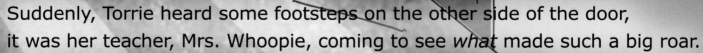

Suddenly, Torrie heard some footsteps on the other side of the door,
it was her teacher, Mrs. Whoopie, coming to see *what* made such a big roar.

Quickly, Torrie rolled a large, white paper cone from a poster she'd torn off the wall,

and placed on top of it, the pink toot, which she had formed into a large, pink, fluffy ball.

Mrs. Whoopie opened the door and was extremely surprised,
to see Torrie Mae Twiddle with a cotton candy that was giant sized.
Mrs. Whoopie said angrily, "Torrie Mae, I'm giving you one minute to
throw away that big treat,
and then come back to the classroom and return to your seat!"

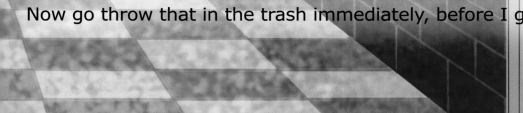

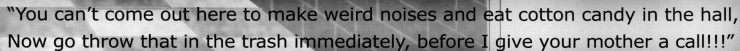

"You can't come out here to make weird noises and eat cotton candy in the hall,
Now go throw that in the trash immediately, before I give your mother a call!!!"

Torrie said, "I'm sorry, Mrs. Whoopie, I promise, it won't happen again",
as Torrie walked down the hall towards the large, green trash bins.
When she reached the trash bins to throw the toot out,
the toot popped up in the air and started floating about.

It stretched itself back into a giant pink cloud of gas,
and started creeping down the hallway, back towards Torrie's class.
All of a sudden, Torrie Mae Twiddle could hear a low grumbling sound,
it was Principal Von Goober mumbling and making his rounds.

Torrie grabbed the pink toot and with no time to spare,
molded the pink toot into a giant, large wig of pink hair.
She placed it on her head as Mr. VonGoober walked by,
he looked at her closely, and then started to sigh,
"The kids these days with their baggy pants and crazy looks,
instead of looking silly, they should be in class reading some books!"

Torrie Mae shrugged her shoulders; Mr. VonGoober gave her a frown,
then he turned the corner of the hallway and continued making his rounds.

Torrie sighed, "Whew, that was close" as she took off her pink hair,
the pink toot re-formed itself into a large pink puff of air.
Torrie waved her hands quickly to fan away the pink pest,
and quickly snuck into the classroom and sat in the very back desk.

The students paid no attention to Torrie Mae, they were listening to the teacher,
when Torrie looked towards the door and saw a pink fluffy creature.
The pink toot turned into a snake and squeezed itself under the door,
and now a long, pink layer of fog was creeping along the classroom floor.

Torrie sprung from her desk and dove onto the ground,
she grabbed the pink toot and rolled it around and around.
The class heard the ruckus and looked towards the door,
and saw Torrie Mae Twiddle rolling around on the floor.

Torrie acted quickly collecting the wandering pink fog,
and molded the pink toot into a fluffy pink poodle dog.
She took off her bracelet she'd bought for a dollar,
and placed it around the pink poodle's neck, pretending it was a collar.

The class screamed with glee, seeing a pink dog in class,
Mrs. Whoopie yelled, "Torrie Mae Twiddle, get rid of that dog...FAST!"
Torrie got off of the floor, and walked the pink toot out into the hall,
when she heard her teacher say, "Go to the principal's office, I'm going to
have to give your mother a call!"

Torrie Mae Twiddle hung her head sadly because she knew she was in trouble, and was wishing that she had never pushed out the giant pink gas bubble.

She walked into VonGoober's office where he yelled, screamed and hollered, and told Torrie that her mom was coming to school, Mrs. Whoopie had already called her.
Torrie didn't own a pink poodle and knew that her mother would be confused, and would have to figure out a way to break her mother the bad news.

So while Torrie Mae Twiddle waited out in the hall,
she formed the pink toot into a fluffy, pink shawl.
She threw the shawl over her shoulders to keep herself warm,
as her mother pulled up quickly, and laid on the horn.

Torrie walked out of the school doors and got into her mom's car,
her mom glared at her and said, "You don't know how disappointed your
father and I are."
"We can't believe that you brought a pink dog to school,
we don't own a pink dog *and* you know it's against the rules."
Torrie rolled her eyes upward, and didn't know what to say,
it would be impossible to explain to her mom what happened today.

Torrie needed some fresh air, so she rolled the window down,
Suddenly, her pink toot shawl started to come all unwound.
The strong breeze pulled the pink toot from around Torrie's neck,
it shot out of the window, and nearly caused a bad wreck.

The pink toot bounced off of a windshield and shot up in the sky,
it rolled and it tumbled as it floated up high.

The pink toot got tangled in the tops of the trees,
but was torn from the branches by a strong, southern breeze.
Higher and higher the pink puff rose up towards the sky,
it looked down at Torrie sadly, and then waved goodbye.
Torrie waved back at the Pink Toot and started feeling kind of sad,
it was definitely one of the most unique toots that she'd ever had.

The Pink Toot is still around; it has not gone,
you can see it during sunsets or at the crack of early dawn.
When the sky shows brilliant color of purple, red, orange and pink,
if you look real closely at the pink cloud, it will give you a friendly wink!